New friends for Flip and
Sam-Boy who tries to te
(with no great success at first), to helpful
Neddy the horse who gets them out of a
tight corner.

New experiences, from first grooming
(traumatic), through the dog-door
(puzzling), to Great Escapes and midnight
capers (almost too exciting)!

Bella is still their best friend, while
Catriona is as irritating (and knowledgeable)
as ever . . .

TONY HICKEY is one of Ireland's leading
authors for children. This is his eighth book
for The Children's Press. The others are:
>
> *The Matchless Mice*
> *The Matchless Mice's Adventure*
> *The Matchless Mice in Space*
> *The Matchless Mice's Space Project*
> *The Black Dog*
> *Flip 'n' Flop*
> *More about Flip 'n' Flop*

He is a trustee of the Irish Children's Book
Trust.

TONY HICKEY

adventures with
Flip'n'Flop

Illustrated by
MARIA MURRAY

THE CHILDREN'S PRESS

First published in 1993 by
The Children's Press
An imprint of Anvil Books
45 Palmerston Road, Dublin 6
Reprinted 1998

ISBN 0 947962 74 3

The moral right of the author has been asserted.

For Monica and Niall
A Special Year

Origination by Computertype
Printed by Colour Books Limited

Contents

1
A New Day

It was a beautiful morning.

Bright sunshine filled the garden as Mrs Johnson opened the doors on to the terrace and let Flip and Flop out of the house.

This was one of the nicest times of the day to the two little dogs. They dashed about in the clear air, sniffing around the trees and the shrubs.

Catriona, the cat, sat on top of the wall and watched them. Then she said, in her lazy voice, 'You don't even know what makes those smells. All kinds of creatures come into your garden at night and you don't know a thing about it! You are fast asleep in your basket!'

Flip and Flop found it very hard not to lose their temper with Catriona when she spoke like this to them.

She made them feel very young and silly.

She made them feel as though they knew nothing.

She made them feel as though they had seen nothing of the great big world.

This, of course, was not true.

Flip and Flop had been born in Scotland. They had come on an airplane to Ireland to live with Frank Johnson.

They had had many adventures with him in his cottage in the Wicklow mountains.

They had had even more adventures when Frank had brought them to live with his parents in their house on the side of the hill close to the sea.

But Catriona seemed to have forgotten all these things as she sat on the wall and looked down at them. 'I am sure that you would like to know the names of some of the creatures that come into your garden at night.'

In spite of feeling cross with Catriona, Flip and Flop had to nod their heads. They could not bear not to know more about these creatures.

'Well,' said Catriona, 'foxes come into your garden at night.'

Flip and Flop did not know what foxes were but there was something about the way that Catriona said the word that made them shiver with excitement.

'They climb over the wall. They have long red tails and pointed ears. They stand in the middle of the garden and look up at the moon. And they walk like this.' Catriona ran along the top of the wall.

'That's not a walk, that's a run,' said Flip. 'I think you are making all this up! I don't believe that any of it is true!'

'Oh it's true all right,' said Catriona. 'Ask Bella.'

Bella, the wise old dog who lived next door with Mr and Mrs Rice, was, at that moment, coming through the gap in the hedge. 'Ask me what?' she asked.

'About foxes,' said Flip. 'Catriona says that they come into this garden during the night.'

'And so they do,' said Bella. 'And badgers as well.'

'"Badgers"? What are badgers?' asked Flop.

'They are black and white animals,' said Bella. 'They live in holes in the ground.'

Holes in the ground! Flip and Flop were amazed by what Bella had told them.

'There are many animals who live in holes in the ground,' continued Bella as she sat down in the shade of the great bush. 'Rabbits, for example.'

Flip and Flop knew about rabbits. They had often chased them when they were taken for walks on the hill. They had never caught any, just seen a flash of a white tail in among the gorse.

'And don't forget the rats and mice,' said Catriona.

'Do rats and mice come into the garden too?' asked Flop. 'It must get very crowded!'

Bella laughed gently. 'No, of course it doesn't get crowded. All the animals would not be here at the same time.'

'You don't know that for sure,' sniffed Catriona. 'You've never seen a garden at night.'

'Yes, I have,' said Bella. 'When I was a young dog, I often used to walk around my garden late at night with Mr Rice. My garden would not be all that different from this one.'

'Maybe not, but when I say "at night" I am talking about the time when all the humans and all the dogs have gone to bed,' said Catriona. 'That is when the wild animals roam.'

'They also roam during the day,' said Flip. 'We've seen rabbits on the hill when we go walking with Frank.'

'And how is Frank?' asked Catriona.

'Still teaching in London,' Flip said sadly.

Frank had written a book that no one

wanted to publish. John, his older brother, had found him a job in a big London school teaching carpentry.

Flip and Flop missed Frank.

They also missed his young brother and sister, Harry and Joan. They were away at boarding-school. They used to take the dogs for lovely long walks. Now the dogs had to depend on Mr and Mrs Johnson.

These walks weren't nearly as long or exciting as the ones with Frank and Joan and Harry.

Mr and Mrs Johnson liked to walk very slowly. They never scrambled over rocks or went down into hollows or jumped across streams.

'We heard Mr and Mrs Johnson talking the other day about Frank and his girlfriend Lucy,' said Flop.

Lucy was an actress. She had given Flip and Flop to Frank. She was now living in London as well.

'Lucy and Frank are going to get married soon,' said Flip.

'Oh, so you know about getting married now, do you?' said Catriona.

'I explained it to them,' said Bella.

'Did you also explain how things might

change when Frank and Lucy are married?' asked the cat. 'Flip and Flop might be in for plenty of surprises!'

Bella glared at Catriona. 'Have you nothing better to do on a nice morning like this than to try and upset Flip and Flop?'

Catriona glared back at Bella. 'I was not trying to upset them. I was just chatting. And, of course, I have something better to do!'

With an angry shake of her sleek head, she jumped down off the wall and vanished from sight.

'I didn't mean to be rude to her,' said Bella, 'but she does get on my nerves sometimes.'

'She gets on our nerves too,' said Flip, 'but what did she mean about things changing when Frank and Lucy get married? Why might there be surprises?'

'Frank might want you to come and live with him,' said Bella. 'In London. Would you like that?'

'He's coming home for something called "half-term",' said Flip.

'That's a holiday,' said Bella. 'Harry and Joan will be home too.'

Flip and Flop felt so happy when they heard this that they forgot all about Catriona and the things that she had said.

'Let's go and sniff around in your garden,' Flop said to Bella.

'All right,' said Bella.

The three dogs made their way towards the gap in the hedge that Mr Rice had made specially for them so that they could go from one garden to the next. Before they got there, Mr Johnson came out on to the terrace and whistled.

'You'd better go and see what he wants,' said Bella. 'I'll wait here.'

'If he is going to take us for a walk we'll let you know so that you can come with us,' Flip said. Then he ran up the garden after Flop.

'Hello there,' said Mr Johnson. He stroked the dogs' ears. When Frank had first brought Flip and Flop to live in the house, Mr Johnson hadn't liked them. Now he was very fond of them.

Mrs Johnson came out of the house and smiled. She was delighted that her husband and the two little border terriers got on so well. She said, 'I suppose it would be better not to give them anything to eat.'

Mr Johnson nodded. 'Yes, that would be best. We don't want them to be sick.'

Flip and Flop looked at each other. The last time a human had said anything like that to them had been in Scotland before they were put on the plane to Dublin.

Was that what was going to happen to them again?

Were Mr and Mrs Johnson going to put them in a big box and take them to the airport?

Were they to be sent to Frank in London?

But that made no sense. Frank was coming back to Ireland soon.

Bella might know the answers to these questions! But, before the border terriers could move, Mr Johnson picked them up and carried them out to where his car was.

The little dogs struggled to get free.

'You would think they knew what was going to happen to them,' said Mrs Johnson as she opened the back door of the car.

'Maybe it is as well that they don't know,' said Mr Johnson. He dumped the dogs on the back seat. Then he closed the door, kissed his wife and drove away from the house.

Flip and Flop could hear Bella barking as the car reached the narrow road that led down to the village.

'What's she saying?' Flip asked.

'I can't quite make it out,' said Flop, 'but it could be "good-bye"!'

'Then she must have known all along what was going to happen to us,' said Flip, 'only she didn't like to tell us.'

'Maybe she didn't know until she saw Mr Johnson pick us up,' said Flop. 'Then it was too late for her to say anything. We will just have to wait and see where Mr Johnson is taking us.'

They looked out of the window at the traffic.

'You don't think we are being taken to live somewhere else, do you?' asked Flip.

That thought gave them such a fright that they flip-flopped down on the back seat and did not move, not even when Mr Johnson stopped the car and opened the back door.

He attached their leads to their collars. 'Come on,' he said. 'Be good now. We are here.'

Then, seeing that the dogs did not want to get out of the car, he reached in and hauled them out on to the pavement.

2

A Strange House

Flip and Flop looked around. They were on a road that they had never seen before. It had rows of trees and rows of nice houses with neat front gardens.

A group of children on their way to school waved at the little dogs.

Flip and Flop tried to wag their tails at them but they were too worried about what was going to happen next.

Mr Johnson made them walk beside him to the door of number seven. He rang the bell and waited. A woman with fair hair opened the door. 'Hello,' she said. 'You must be Mr Johnson. And these must be Flip and Flop!'

'That's right,' said Mr Johnson. 'And you must be Mrs Joyce. If you don't mind, I won't delay. I'm late for the office as it is.'

'I quite understand,' said Mrs Joyce. She took the leads.

'Be good,' Mr Johnson said to the dogs. Then he went back to his car and drove off.

'It's happened!' said Flip. 'We've been given away!'

'Not only that,' said Flop, 'but we've been given away to someone that Mr Johnson had never met before! That's why he and Mrs Joyce had to tell each other their names.'

'Well, aren't you the chatty dogs!' said Mrs Joyce. She gently tugged the leads and made the dogs go into the house with her.

When she had closed the front door, she took the leads off and looked at the dogs.

'Not too bad,' she said. 'As soon as my husband has gone, I'll get started on you.'

A door at the end of the hall opened. A man with a briefcase came out of the kitchen. He glanced at Flip and Flop. 'What kind are these?' he asked.

'Border terriers,' said Mrs Joyce.

'How many does that make this week?'

'Seven,' said Mrs Joyce.

Seven! Flip and Flop could hardly believe their ears. Mrs Joyce had been given seven dogs in one week! But where were the other five? Had something terrible happened to them?

'We'll have to try and get away from here,' Flip whispered.

'How can we do that?' asked Flop.

'That man must be Mr Joyce,' replied Flip. 'I think he is going to the office. That means he will have to open the front door. Get ready to run for it!'

Flop began to tremble. He hated it when things got too exciting. 'Where will we go when we get outside?' he whispered.

Flip had no time to answer this before Mr Joyce reached for the door-latch. 'See you later,' he said to his wife.

'All right,' said Mrs Joyce. 'I should have finished with these two by lunch-time!'

Flop stopped trembling. Finish with himself and Flop by lunch-time! How dare Mrs Joyce talk about them like that!'

He moved closer to Flip, who had moved closer to Mr Joyce.

Mr Joyce began to pull back the latch.

Then he stood on Flip's front left paw!

In spite of himself, Flip yelped with pain. 'Oh, I'm sorry,' said Mr Joyce.

'Don't worry, he'll be all right in a few seconds,' said Mrs Joyce. She caught the dogs by their collars. 'They should know by now not to get under people's feet!'

Before Flip and Flop could even try to wriggle free, Mr Joyce opened the front door and went out of the house. The front door closed with a loud click.

'Now what are we to do?' keened Flop.

'It's all my fault, getting in Mr Joyce's way,' cried Flip.

'No, no, don't blame yourself.' said Flop.

'Honestly, I've never known such chatty dogs!' said Mrs Joyce. She carried them out into the back garden. 'You should be fine here until I'm ready for you.'

As soon as Mrs Joyce had closed the back door, Flip and Flop looked anxiously around for a way out of the garden. There were walls instead of hedges.

'These walls are too high for us,' said Flop.

Then a black and white dog jumped over the wall and landed in the garden.

'Hello there,' he said to Flip and Flop.

'How did you jump over a wall that high?' asked Flop.

'It's just something I can do,' said the dog.

'Could you teach us how to do it?' asked Flip.

'I don't think it is something that you can learn,' said the dog, 'but I can show you how to do it.'

He stood still for a moment. Then he rushed forward, soared up in the air and landed on top of the wall. 'Now you try it,' he said to Flip and Flop.

The two little border terriers stood in the

same place as the dog had stood. Then together they rushed forward towards the wall. But something went wrong.

Instead of soaring through the air, they crashed into each other and rolled over on the grass.

'Maybe you should try it one at a time,' said the dog.

'You go first,' Flop said to Flip.

'All right,' said Flip. 'Stand back! Give me plenty of room!'

Flop moved far out of Flip's way. Flip stood in the same place as before. He waited until he felt ready. Then he ran as fast as he could towards the wall. But the closer he got to the wall, the higher it seemed to become.

Also, his feet just would not leave the ground. Instead of landing on top of the wall, he crashed into it!

'You waited too long before you jumped,' said the dog. 'Let your friend try.'

'He's my brother, not my friend,' said Flip.

'All right then, so he's your brother. What's his name?'

'Flop,' said Flip. 'And I'm Flip.'

'And I'm Sam-Boy,' said the dog on the wall.

'Before I jump, I want to ask you something,' said Flop. 'Do you often come around here?'

'Oh yes,' said Sam-Boy, 'I come and visit here almost every day. There are always dogs for me to talk to.'

'But what happens to those dogs?' asked Flip.

'What do you mean "happens"?'

'What does Mrs Joyce, the woman in the house, do with them?'

'I don't know,' said Sam-Boy. 'What makes you think that she does anything with them? But wait a minute . . . there *is* one strange thing . . .'

'And what is that?' Flop asked. He felt himself beginning to tremble again.

'I never saw any of them more than once,' said Sam-Boy. 'They are here in the morning, but when I come back in the afternoon there is no sign of them anywhere. Every morning there is a new lot. Just like you today.'

'Do you mean that they just disappear?' asked Flip.

'Yes, I suppose that is what I mean!'

'You mean we won't be here this afternoon?' Flip's voice trembled.

'I'm afraid so.'

This news was too much for Flop. He

threw back his head and keened.

Flip wanted to be very brave. But he just could not help but join in with Flop. He began to keen as well.

'Someone is coming,' Sam-Boy said and jumped down into the next garden.

The back door of the house opened. Mrs Joyce came out. '*Now* what is the matter? I had to tidy the kitchen before I set to work on the two of you. But now I am ready, so one at a time!' She looked at Flop. 'You'd better be first!'

Flop tried to get away by running around the garden but Mrs Joyce caught him easily.

'Help me! Help me!' he called out to Flip.

Flip jumped around Mrs Joyce. He barked and he growled. But Mrs Joyce just laughed as she carried Flop into the house and closed the back door.

Sam-Boy was back on top of the wall. 'What happened?' he asked.

'She's taken Flop,' said Flip. 'We've never been separated before! Oh what can she be doing to him?'

'Unfortunately I can't see through the curtains,' said Sam-Boy. 'But let's listen. Maybe we'll hear something.'

Flip and Sam-Boy listened. There was no

sound from inside the house.

'You'll have to go and get help,' said Flip. 'Bring as many dogs as you can around to the front door.'

'All right,' said Sam-Boy. 'I'll do my best.'

Once more, Sam-Boy jumped down into his own garden. He found his way out on to the road. He raced along it, calling out, 'Dogs in danger! Help! Help! Dogs in danger!'

From behind closed gates and from inside houses dogs called back, 'What do you mean? What do you mean?'

Humans clapped hands over their ears and shouted, 'Stop that noise! Stop that noise!'

A man, mowing his lawn, threw a stone at Sam-Boy. 'Clear off! Go home!' he said.

Sam-Boy ran into the next road and the next and the next, but the only dog who managed to get out and follow him was a battered-looking mongrel with very short legs. 'What's going on?' she asked.

'Dogs in danger over at the Joyces,' panted Sam-Boy.

'The Joyces!' said the mongrel. 'You'll never manage to get a dog out of that house. They always arrive and leave in motor-cars.' She turned away.

'Where are you going?' asked Sam-Boy.

'Home,' said the mongrel. 'So will you, if you have any sense.'

'No, I can't do that yet,' said Sam-Boy. 'I have to go back and let Flip know that I, at least, tried to help him.'

Sam-Boy ran back along the roads, through the garden and jumped back on to the wall.

Flip was sniffing under the back door and giving plaintive little barks.

'Has anything happened?' asked Sam-Boy.

'No,' said Flip sadly.

'I'm afraid I didn't do much good either,'

said Sam-Boy. 'The humans around here keep their dogs locked up.'

'They're afraid they'll get run over,' said Flip, remembering Frank.

The back door opened. Mrs Joyce came out. She had a blue and white apron on over her frock. 'Your turn now,' she said.

'Best go in,' said Sam-Boy. 'You might find out what's happened to Flop.'

Flip went slowly into the house. His tail drooped. His ears were down. He looked up sadly at Mrs Joyce. 'Such a sad dog!' she said. 'You won't know yourself by the time I've finished with you!'

'That is exactly what I am afraid of,' thought Flip.

Mrs Joyce brought him into a room. There was a basin filled with water on the floor, and a white table with shiny things on it. It looked like the table at the vet's.

'First the clip. Then the cut. Then the wash. Then the whizoo!' said Mrs Joyce.

She lifted Flip up on to the table, picked up a pair of scissors and a comb and set to work.

She snipped and combed and clipped and shaved his coat. She turned him this way and that until he felt quite dizzy. Then she popped him into the basin and shampooed him until he felt too ticklish to be frightened.

Then came the whizoo. It was long and shiny and blew hot air all over him. Flip didn't like this at all. 'Stop it!' he yelled.

'Honestly such a baby, afraid of a hair-dryer,' said Mrs Joyce. 'Flop didn't mind at all!'

So this was what had happened to Flop! But where was he now?

Mrs Joyce smoothed Flip's coat with a towel. 'Now who's a pretty boy!' she said. As soon as she opened the door of the room, Flip dashed out into the hall. 'Flop? Flop?' he called. 'Where are you?'

'I'm in here,' Flop called back.

Mrs Joyce opened the door of another room.

Flop was sitting in a pool of bright sun-shine in the middle of the room.

The two little dogs rushed towards each other.

'Honestly,' said Mrs Joyce. 'You would think you hadn't seen each other for years! Stay here now and be good.' Then she closed the door.

'We can hardly go anywhere if we are locked in,' grumbled Flip. Then he stared at

'I suppose we will have to stay clean now,' said Flip.

'Well do your best until Mr Johnson comes back,' said Bella. 'You are lucky that Mrs Johnson can drive Frank's car. Otherwise you would have had to stay at Mrs Joyce's until Mr Johnson was finished in his office.'

'Mrs Johnson said there were workmen coming later on today,' said Flip.

'Oh, I wonder what they are going to do,' said Bella.

The dogs did not have to wait very long before finding out.

A half an hour later a van drove down the drive. Two men, one wearing brown overalls, the other wearing blue jeans and a blue shirt, got out. Mrs Johnson was delighted to see them. 'You are nice and early,' she said. 'I hope that means that you can get the job done before my husband gets home. He hates noise.'

'We will do our best,' said the man in the overalls. 'Where is the door to go?'

'Come out through the kitchen and I will show you,' said Mrs Johnson.

Bella and the terriers had arrived on the terrace in time to hear the conversation.

They looked in through the big glass

Flop. His brother looked quite different. He was all neat and tidy.

Flop looked at Flip. He was thinking the very same thing. 'Maybe she did it so that no one will know us,' he said.

'It's all very worrying,' said Flip.

They heard a car pull up outside the house. They heard footsteps on the garden path. Then the doorbell rang.

'That could be someone to take us away,' said Flip.

There was a murmur of voices. Then the door of the room opened. In came Mrs Joyce with – and here Flip and Flop thought they were seeing things – none other than Mrs Johnson!

The women roared with laughter. 'I have never seen two dogs look so surprised,' said Mrs Joyce.

The two little dogs flung themselves at Mrs Johnson. 'It's you!' they said. 'It really is you!'

'They must have thought we were giving them away,' said Mrs Johnson. She bent down and petted Flip and Flop.

Mrs Joyce came back with their leads and slipped them on to their collars.

'They look splendid ,' Mrs Johnson said.

'Thank you very much. I have a cheque here for you.'

'Thanks,' said Mrs Joyce, putting the cheque into her apron pocket.

Mrs Johnson walked the dogs out of the house to where Frank's car was. 'It's my son's car,' she explained. 'He's in London. The dogs are his too. He'll be delighted when he sees them looking so nice.'

Flip and Flop did a little dance. They were not being given away at all. They were being got ready for Frank's home-coming.

'It was very good of you to do them so quickly,' Mrs Johnson said. 'I have workmen coming later on today. Is that one of your dogs?' She pointed to Sam-Boy who had just come running around the corner.

'No,' said Mrs Joyce. 'I don't know who he belongs to. He's always around the place.'

Sam-Boy reached the car as Flip and Flop were put on the back seat.

'Where are you being taken?' he asked.

'Home,' said the border terriers. 'We are being taken back to the house on the hill close to the sea. Thank you for trying to help us. Thank you! Thank you!'

3
A New Door

As soon as they got home, Mrs Johns Flip and Flop a special breakfast, wh gobbled down. All the excitement an of the morning had made them very

Then she let them out into the gard

Bella was waiting for them unde bush. She looked very carefully 'You've been groomed,' she said. ' nice you look too!'

'We were afraid that we were bei away,' said Flop.

Bella listened to all that had h Then she said, 'You know now why never saw the other dogs again.'

'We were just going to ask you al said Flip.

'It's because Mrs Joyce put the front room so that they would stay clean until their humans came for t

'Of course!' said Flop. 'That's were put there too. It was so that be nice and clean when Mrs Johr for us.'

Flop. His brother looked quite different. He was all neat and tidy.

Flop looked at Flip. He was thinking the very same thing. 'Maybe she did it so that no one will know us,' he said.

'It's all very worrying,' said Flip.

They heard a car pull up outside the house. They heard footsteps on the garden path. Then the doorbell rang.

'That could be someone to take us away,' said Flip.

There was a murmur of voices. Then the door of the room opened. In came Mrs Joyce with – and here Flip and Flop thought they were seeing things – none other than Mrs Johnson!

The women roared with laughter. 'I have never seen two dogs look so surprised,' said Mrs Joyce.

The two little dogs flung themselves at Mrs Johnson. 'It's you!' they said. 'It really is you!'

'They must have thought we were giving them away,' said Mrs Johnson. She bent down and petted Flip and Flop.

Mrs Joyce came back with their leads and slipped them on to their collars.

'They look splendid ,' Mrs Johnson said.

'Thank you very much. I have a cheque here for you.'

'Thanks,' said Mrs Joyce, putting the cheque into her apron pocket.

Mrs Johnson walked the dogs out of the house to where Frank's car was. 'It's my son's car,' she explained. 'He's in London. The dogs are his too. He'll be delighted when he sees them looking so nice.'

Flip and Flop did a little dance. They were not being given away at all. They were being got ready for Frank's home-coming.

'It was very good of you to do them so quickly,' Mrs Johnson said. 'I have workmen coming later on today. Is that one of your dogs?' She pointed to Sam-Boy who had just come running around the corner.

'No,' said Mrs Joyce. 'I don't know who he belongs to. He's always around the place.'

Sam-Boy reached the car as Flip and Flop were put on the back seat.

'Where are you being taken?' he asked.

'Home,' said the border terriers. 'We are being taken back to the house on the hill close to the sea. Thank you for trying to help us. Thank you! Thank you!'

3
A New Door

As soon as they got home, Mrs Johnson gave Flip and Flop a special breakfast, which they gobbled down. All the excitement and worry of the morning had made them very hungry.

Then she let them out into the garden.

Bella was waiting for them under the big bush. She looked very carefully at them. 'You've been groomed,' she said. 'And very nice you look too!'

'We were afraid that we were being given away,' said Flop.

Bella listened to all that had happened. Then she said, 'You know now why Sam-Boy never saw the other dogs again.'

'We were just going to ask you about that,' said Flip.

'It's because Mrs Joyce put them in that front room so that they would stay nice and clean until their humans came for them.'

'Of course!' said Flop. 'That's why we were put there too. It was so that we would be nice and clean when Mrs Johnson came for us.'

'I suppose we will have to stay clean now,' said Flip.

'Well do your best until Mr Johnson comes back,' said Bella. 'You are lucky that Mrs Johnson can drive Frank's car. Otherwise you would have had to stay at Mrs Joyce's until Mr Johnson was finished in his office.'

'Mrs Johnson said there were workmen coming later on today,' said Flip.

'Oh, I wonder what they are going to do,' said Bella.

The dogs did not have to wait very long before finding out.

A half an hour later a van drove down the drive. Two men, one wearing brown overalls, the other wearing blue jeans and a blue shirt, got out. Mrs Johnson was delighted to see them. 'You are nice and early,' she said. 'I hope that means that you can get the job done before my husband gets home. He hates noise.'

'We will do our best,' said the man in the overalls. 'Where is the door to go?'

'Come out through the kitchen and I will show you,' said Mrs Johnson.

Bella and the terriers had arrived on the terrace in time to hear the conversation.

They looked in through the big glass

windows as Mrs Johnson took the two workmen out into the dogs' room where their
basket was.

'I didn't notice that there was anything
wrong with the door in there,' said Flop.

'Neither did I,' said Flip.

Mrs Johnson and the workmen came back
into the kitchen. She pointed at Flip and
Flop. 'There they are,' she said. She opened
the doors and held her hand out for the
terriers to come to her.

'They won't bite, will they?' asked the man
in blue.

'Of course they won't,' said Mrs Johnson.
'Anyway, I'll be holding them.' She told Flip
and Flop to stand still. The man in the
overalls took a piece of wood with marks on
it and held it against each of the dogs. Then
he wrote something down in a notebook.
Then the border terriers were let out and the
doors were closed.

'What was all that about?' asked Flip.

'Beats me,' said Bella.

'Dog-door,' said a voice that they all knew.

They looked around. Catriona was sitting
on the edge of the terrace.

'Dog-door?' said Flop. 'What do you mean
by that?'

'It is a special door that humans put in other doors so that dogs can get in and out of the house by themselves,' said Catriona. 'I just happened to be sitting on top of the shed and heard what Mrs Johnson and the workmen were saying.'

Bella and the border terriers knew that Catriona hadn't arrived on top of the garden shed by accident. She had chosen the spot deliberately so that she could listen to Mrs Johnson and the workmen. That was how she and her cat friends found out things. They sat on sheds and window ledges-and slipped silently in and out of gardens and listened.

'The workman in the overalls was measuring you just now to make sure that the door would be big enough for you to get through,' explained Catriona.

'But the door in our room only goes out into the yard,' said Flip.

'Well you could hardly expect them to cut a hole in the glass doors on to the terrace,' said Catriona.

'I don't see why they have to cut a hole . . . I mean make a dog-door at all,' said Flip.

'Neither do I,' said Flop.

'I could tell you,' said Catriona. 'And I

would if I could be sure that you wouldn't get cross with me.'

'Is it any wonder we do get cross when you tease us like this?' said Bella. 'If you have something to tell us, why don't you say it straight out like a . . . a dog would?'

'Because I am not a dog. I'm a cat. And I have only two words to say to you. And those are the words that I said to you earlier today. Changes and surprises!'

Catriona stretched lazily and flicked her tail. 'Changes and surprises! Remember those words. Changes and surprises!' Then she jumped down off the terrace and walked slowly down the garden.

Bella growled angrily. She thought that Catriona was teasing them again. But Flip and Flop were certain that Catriona knew something very important. They hurried after her.

'Please, Catriona,' said Flop. 'Tell us what you know.'

Catriona looked at them with her pale green eyes. 'You are old enough to work things out for yourselves.'

'No, we aren't,' said Flip, forgetting that he and Flop had once promised never to be too friendly with cats.

'Well then, ask yourselves a few questions,' said Catriona. 'Why would you and your brother need a dog-door at all?'

'You told us the answer to that already,' said Flop. 'It is so that we can get in and out of the house by ourselves.'

'And why would you want to do that?'

Flop suddenly knew the answer. 'We would want to do that if we were in the house all by ourselves.'

'Exactly right,' said Catriona.

'But we are never in the house by ourselves, except, maybe, when Mrs Johnson is out shopping. Or she and Mr Johnson go for a drive,' said Flop.

'Supposing that were to change,' said Catriona. 'Supposing you were to be left alone all day!'

'Why would that happen?' asked Flop.

'Golf!' said Catriona.

'Golf?' said Flip and Flop. 'What's "golf"?'

'Golf is what makes things change!' said Catriona. Then she jumped over the wall and vanished.

Flip and Flop were so amazed by what Catriona had said that they just flopped down in the shade of the big bush. Bella came and lay beside them. 'What did

Catriona tell you?' she asked.

'She said we might be left alone all day because of something called "golf",' said Flip.

'Oh dear . . . she could be right! Have you seen any big leather bags in your house? Tall bags with things sticking out of the top?'

'Yes,' said Flop. 'Mr Johnson brought home two bags like that the other day.'

'They are golf-bags. The things in them are golf-clubs. Humans take the bags and the clubs to special places called golf courses. They use the clubs to hit little white balls into little round holes,' said Bella. 'There is a golf course very near here. Mr and Mrs Johnson must be going to play golf!'

'But it wouldn't take them all day to hit a ball into a hole, would it?' asked Flip.

'It could,' said Bella. 'A dog friend of mine told me that her humans play golf. They are away for hours at a time.'

'I don't like the idea of spending hours in the backyard,' said Flop. 'It's boring.'

The backyard of the house was small. The ground was hard, cold cement. The only thing to be seen from it was a corner of the rockery. And that could only be seen by looking through some wire.

'It might not be as bad as you think,' said Bella.

'No,' said Flop. 'It will probably be worse!'

There was a rustle in the branches above their heads. They looked up and saw Catriona smiling down at them. 'I forgot to say how lovely you both look after your haircuts. You look like two little kittens!'

This was just too much for Flip and Flop. They jumped up and barked and shouted and yelled. Among the things they yelled was, 'You stay out of our garden!'

But both they and Bella and Catriona knew that when she came back they would not be able to stop asking her questions. Catriona knew too many things.

All the same, the border terriers felt better when they had finished barking and jumping. They settled down again beside Bella and listened to the sound of hammering and sawing coming from the house.

The noise went on for a long time. Finally it stopped.

Then Mrs Johnson opened the door on to the terrace and called to Flip and Flop. They weren't very happy about going to her but there was nothing else that they could do.

They followed her into the room where

their basket was. A new small door had been set into a panel of the back door.

'Now then,' said Mrs Johnson. 'Just watch me. This is a dog-door.'

She pushed the dog-door. It swung open.

She took her hand away. The dog-door snapped shut with a bang!

Flip and Flop jumped back.

'Oh dear,' said Mrs Johnson. 'That didn't go very well.' She opened the back door and spoke to the two workmen in the yard. 'The dog-door closes too quickly.'

'That's because it's new,' said the man in the overalls. 'The hinges will loosen after a while. Try it from this side!'

Mrs Johnson went out into the yard, bent down and tried the door from that side. It seemed to work slightly better.

'Now push the dogs through,' said the man in blue.

'Push us through! What cheek!' thought Flip.

Mrs Johnson came back into the house, closed the back door and gave Flip a shove forward. Flip tried to get a grip on the floor but the tiles were too shiny. He slid along until he was pressed up against the dog-door. Mrs Johnson gave him one last shove.

Flip was out of the house and into the yard!

The man in blue said, 'He'll soon get the hang of it!'

Then Flop was pushed through into the yard. The dog-door slammed shut again.

'I hate the noise it makes,' said Flop.

'So do I,' said Flip.

Mrs Johnson called, 'Come back in, Flip! Come back in, Flop!'

Flip sighed. 'We'd better do as she asks.' He went forward and pushed the dog-door with his head. It opened very slowly.

'There you are,' said the workmen. 'I knew they'd get the hang of it. If you've any problems, just telephone us.'

'Very well,' said Mrs Johnson.

The workmen put their tools back into the van. 'Good-bye,' they said and drove off.

Flip and Flop went back into the yard and looked at the dog-door.

Bella came scrambling across the rockery and looked through the wire at Flip and Flop. 'How are you getting on?' she asked.

'It's too soon to tell,' said Flip.

'I wonder how many other surprises there are going to be,' said Flop.

Mrs Johnson came back to talk to them. 'I am going to leave you a nice bowl of water out here,' she said. 'You will have plenty of shade. And you can always go into your basket if you get tired of the yard.'

'We are tired of the yard already,' said Flip. But, of course, Mrs Johnson didn't understand. She just smiled and put down the bowl of water. Then she locked the back door.

Bella looked around the corner of the house. She saw Mrs Johnson come out of the house with her bag of golf-clubs and put them into Frank's car. 'She won't be back for ages,' thought Bella. But she did not say this to Flip and Flop. The little dogs had had enough excitement for one day.

4

A Discovery

Flip and Flop sat in the middle of the yard. Bella had gone home to make sure that everything was all right at her house. She had promised to be back soon but that had been a long time ago.

'Something must have happened to delay her,' said Flip.

'Maybe Mr and Mrs Rice have taken her for a walk,' said Flip.

Mr and Mrs Rice did not often go for walks. When they did, they walked even more slowly than Mr and Mrs Johnson.

'We haven't had our walk yet today,' said Flip.

'Maybe going to have our hair cut is the same thing as going for a walk to humans,' said Flop.

'Well, it's not the same thing to me,' grumbled Flip. 'And another thing, will we not get all dirty out here in this yard? It is covered with dust.'

'Why don't you go back into your basket?' a familiar voice called.

The dogs looked up. Catriona was on the garden shed, looking down at them.

'Because we like it better out here,' Flip said crossly.

Catriona's eyes twinkled. 'Are you sure it is not just because you forgot that you can use the dog-door whenever you want to go inside?'

'Of course, it isn't,' said Flip.

'Maybe it is because you don't like the noise that the door makes,' said Catriona.

Flip and Flop looked at each other. Catriona had been listening to every word that had been said.

What was even more annoying was that what Catriona had said was true. Flip and Flop had forgotten that they could go into their basket by using the dog-door.

'Don't say anything at all to her,' whispered Flop. 'Don't let her annoy you. She'll soon go away.'

Flip nodded and lay down on the ground as though it was as soft as the towel in their basket.

'Time for naps for the little dogs, is it?' said Catriona. "Well I suppose you've had a very busy day. Of course, if you were a cat you would not think of sleeping. You would be too busy trying to escape.'

In spite of not wanting to talk to Catriona, the two little dogs just could not pretend that they had not heard what she had said.

Catriona, knowing quite well what they were thinking, said, 'I am not being fair when I say that only cats try to escape when they are locked in. I know a few dogs who have managed to get out of their prison.'

Until that moment, Flip and Flop had never thought of themselves as being in prison. Yet, in a way, the yard must be exactly what humans meant when they spoke of prison.

Flip and Flop had often heard Mr Johnson say, when something on the news upset him, 'They should lock that lot up in prison.'

But Flip and Flop had done nothing wrong. If anything, they had been as good as gold for almost three days.

'It is very easy to escape when you know how,' said Catriona. 'But still, since you say you are happy in this yard, I have nothing else to say to you. I think I'll go and visit my friends at the new Quarry Hotel. There is a big wedding there today. That means lots of delicious scraps. We may even have a sing-song later on.'

'I hope it is better than the last one you had,' said Flip, forgetting that he wasn't going to say a word to Catriona. 'That sounded as though you and your friends had a tummy-ache.'

Catriona laughed her annoying cat laugh. 'And what would two border terriers, who cannot even get out of a yard, know about cat music? Cat music just happens to be the most magical in the world.'

With that, Catriona jumped down off the shed into the field next door.

'Oh,' said Flip. 'She does make me cross.'

'Me too,' said Flop. 'We will just have to learn not to pay her any attention.'

'I know, I know,' said Flip. 'But she does think that she is our friend. Even worse, though, is the fact that almost everything she says is so interesting.'

'Do you mean like us trying to escape from the yard?' asked Flop.

'That is exactly what I mean,' said Flip, 'only I don't see how we could do that.'

'Even if we could escape, would we want to?' Flop asked nervously.

'I think it might be rather nice,' said Flip. 'Let's have a look around.'

The two little dogs looked at the door out

into the big garden. There seemed to be no way that they could open that.

The same thing was true of the door to the front of the house.

'Maybe we could scrape our way through them,' said Flip. 'The wood isn't very thick.'

'And what would Mr Johnson say if we did that?' asked Flop. 'He has only started to like us. If we make a hole in one of the doors, he might really give us away.'

'That's true,' said Flip. 'But there must be some way out.'

'Maybe Catriona was just teasing us.'

'No, I don't think that she was. I think that she was telling us that there was a way out of this yard. It is up to us to find it.' Then he noticed something odd about one piece of the wire that separated the yard from the rockery. He ran over to it.

'What have you found?' asked Flop.

'This piece of wire here doesn't go all the way down to the ground,' said Flip. He touched it with his nose. The wire moved. 'It's loose!'

Flop stopped feeling nervous. Instead, he felt excited. 'This must be what Catriona was talking about!' He pushed the wire with his nose.

The wire moved again.

Together the two dogs pushed at it. It lifted a tiny bit.

Together they pushed their noses further under the wire.

The wire lifted even more.

The two dogs wriggled and pushed even harder.

Suddenly they could wriggle all the way under the wire and out on to the rockery.

'We've done it!' cried Flip. 'We've escaped!'

Suddenly Flop stopped feeling excited. He went back to being nervous. 'Now what are we going to do?' he asked.

'We are going to go for the walk that we didn't have,' said Flip.

'What if Mrs Johnson comes home? She could get very cross if we aren't in the yard.'

'Mrs Johnson won't be back for hours and hours.' It was Catriona who spoke, sitting on the roof of the garage. Two cats that the dogs had never seen before were with her.

Flip and Flop said nothing. They were not going to pay any attention to Catriona.

'Aren't they sweet?' Catriona said to the other two cats. 'They like to pretend that they don't want to talk to me. They even like to pretend that they don't want to listen to me. Yet they do everything that I tell them to do!'

'We most certainly do not!' said Flip, once more forgetting he wasn't going to talk.

'You escaped from the yard, didn't you?' said Catriona. 'You would not have done that if I hadn't told you about it. And now you want to know how I know that Mrs Johnson will not be home for hours and hours.'

'You are just guessing,' said Flip.

'No, I'm not,' said Catriona. 'My two friends here told me. They live near the golf course. They saw Mrs Johnson there.'

'She was just starting her game,' one of the cats said. 'She hadn't even managed to hit the ball while we were watching her.'

'I don't know why we are wasting our time with these dogs,' said the second cat. 'They seem to be very stupid to me. And anyway if we don't hurry, we will be late for the wedding at the Quarry Hotel.'

The two strange cats jumped off the garage and landed just a few feet away from Flip and Flop.

The two dogs began to growl.

'Oh be quiet,' said the first cat. 'You couldn't catch us if you had wings!'

46

And that was when the chase started!

Up the drive went the two cats with the two dogs after them.

They dodged in and out through the pine-trees at the gate. Then the cats jumped over the wall and out on to the road.

Flip and Flop ran after them. They almost knocked Mr Rice down. He yelled at them.

Bella, who was with him, ran after the dogs. 'Where are you going?' she asked. 'How did you get out of the yard?'

'We escaped,' Flip shouted. 'Now we are chasing these two cats! They said we were stupid!'

'And perhaps they are right,' said Bella.

Flip and Flop were so surprised at this that they stopped running.

'You'll never catch those cats,' said Bella. 'I should know. I've tried often enough.'

By now the cats were nowhere to be seen. They had disappeared into one of the other gardens.

'You'd better come back with me,' said Bella. 'Mr Rice is waiting.'

The three dogs walked back to where Mr Rice was. 'Now how did you two get out on to the road?' he asked Flip and Flop.

The two border terriers became very worried. Mr Rice would tell the Johnsons what had happened. They could get into trouble!

Fortunately at that moment, Mrs Rice came to her front gate. 'What on earth was all that racket?' she asked. 'It sounded like a dog fight?'

'It was Flip and Flop chasing cats,' said Mr Rice, 'but how did they get out on to the road?'

'Oh dear,' said Mrs Rice. 'Maybe it was my fault. I decided to weed under the rose-trees while you and Bella were down at the village. I must have left the side gate open.

That's how they got out. We had better not say anything to Mrs Johnson. Otherwise she would not let Flip and Flop out into the garden by themselves again.'

'That's true,' said Mr Rice. 'Just be a bit more careful in future!'

Flip and Flop followed Bella into the Rices' back garden. Then the three of them jumped through the gap in the hedge and settled down under the big bush.

'Well you are very lucky dogs,' said Bella. 'Poor Mrs Rice thinks that it is her fault that you were out on the road. Neither she nor Mr Rice will say anything to your people.'

Flip and Flop nodded. Flop said, 'All's well that ends well.' Then he stopped feeling happy. 'Only it has not ended well at all. Flip and I should be back in the yard, not out here in the garden. We should never have listened to Catriona!'

'It's a bit too late to say that now,' said Bella. 'This is a real mess!'

5

Neddy to the Rescue

'Well,' said Bella after a while. 'No good will come from keening over lost bones. We have to find a way of getting you back into the yard.'

Without thinking, Flip and Flop looked at the wall behind them. They had become so used to Catriona appearing at moments like this that they expected to hear her voice. But there was no sign of the cat. She was obviously down at the Quarry Hotel with her friends.

'Surely there is a way out of this garden into the field next door?' asked Flip. 'If there was, we could get back into the yard the same way as we got out.'

'Let's look,' said Bella.

The three dogs began to examine the long wall that separated the garden of the Johnsons from the field next to it.

They were almost back at the terrace when Bella said, 'Come and look at this.'

Bella pointed to a small hole in the wall, hidden from view behind a huge rose-bush.

'It's a possibility,' said Flip. He touched the hole with his front paw. The soil slipped into the field, making the hole bigger. 'We might fit through here,' he said.

'It could be dangerous,' said Bella. 'I think that the roots of that tree there . . .' Flip and Flop looked at the tree that leaned over the top of the wall '. . . have grown underneath the wall. That's what has made the hole. But if we're not very careful, the whole wall could come tumbling down.'

'I'll be very careful,' said Flip.

He lay as flat as he could on the ground. He stretched his front legs out in front of him and his back legs out behind him. Then he moved slowly forward.

His head went through the hole easily enough. Then his shoulders and the rest of his body. But he was not prepared for the big drop between the garden and the field.

He went sliding down like someone on a slide. He bumped and banged against rocks and gorse-bushes. He rolled over and over and finally came to a stop in a clump of buttercups.

He lay there, too frightened to move. Then he remembered what Bella had said about the wall tumbling down.

If that happened, all the stones and clay would land on him!

He managed to stand up.

Bella and Flop called out through the gap in the wall. 'Flip! Flip! Are you all right?'

'Yes. Yes, I think so,' Flip called back. 'But what about the wall? Will it not come tumbling down?'

Before Flop or Bella could answer, there was a loud thundering noise. For a terrible moment, Flip thought that the whole garden and not just the wall was going to tumble into the field.

He turned to get as far away as he could from the danger and almost bumped into a horse!

'Hello,' said the horse. 'My name is Neddy. What's happening here?'

'My brother and I are trying to get through the hole in the garden wall,' said Flip. 'I just about managed it. But Flop, that's my brother, is a bit fatter. He might make the wall come tumbling down.'

'Let me see if I can help,' said Neddy. He made his way to a place where the drop down into the field was not too high. He carefully balanced himself there and stuck his head over the garden wall. He saw Bella and Flop looking through the hole in the wall. They were trying to see what was happening in the field.

'Hello there, Bella,' Neddy said.

Bella raised her head and looked at the horse. She was delighted to see him. 'Hello, Neddy,' she said. 'I didn't know you were back.'

'I arrived back just a few minutes ago,' he said. 'I've been down in the country since Easter. But what's going on with these two friends of yours?'

Bella quickly told him while Flop just sat and stared at Neddy. The last time he had spoken to a horse had been when he and Flip lived with Frank in the cottage.

Neddy shook his head when Bella had finished. 'Cats and dogs running around the road like that!'

'Chasing cats is often something that dogs just have to do,' said Bella. 'I used to do it myself when I was a pup. But now, can you help Flip and Flop to get back into the yard?'

'Yes, of course I can,' said Neddy. 'Just send young Flop down here to me.'

Bella nodded at Flop to come closer.

'Push him up the wall a bit,' said Neddy.

Bella shoved Flop as hard as she could. Neddy leaned down over the wall and caught Flop by his collar. Then he swung Flop over the wall and put him down gently into the field.

Flop had never felt so nervous in his life. But he managed to say, 'Thank you, Neddy.'

'Plenty of time for thanks later on,' said Neddy. 'Follow me and I'll show you and your brother how to get back on to the rockery.'

The two little dogs ran alongside Neddy until they came to a scraggly-looking hedge. 'It doesn't grow too well because of the rocky ground,' said Neddy. 'You should have no trouble squeezing through it.'

Neddy was right. Flip and Flop found the hedge very easy to squeeze through. They came out on to the rockery. Then they only had to crawl under the wire to get back into the yard.

'Wow!' said Flop, flopping down on the ground. 'Now I really can say that "All's well, that ends well".'

Flip said, 'Maybe what you really should say is that "All's well that BEGINS well".'

'Begins? What do you mean by "begins well"?' Flop was feeling nervous again. He didn't like the look on Flip's face.

'I mean that we have made a very important discovery today,' said Flip. 'We now know how to get in and out of the yard. We also know how to get in and out of the field.'

'Why would we want to get in and out of the field?'

'So that we can talk to Neddy and find out

what he was doing down the country. Would you not like to know that?'

'Yes, I would,' said Flop. 'I would also like to know why he lives in that field.'

Bella climbed over the rockery. 'Push the wire down,' she said. 'You don't want the Johnsons to know that you lifted it.'

Flip and Flop did as she told them.

Then Flop began to worry again. 'What will Mr and Mrs Rice think when they see that we are not in the back garden?'

'They will be going out soon to the cinema,' said Bella. 'That's why Mr Rice went down to the village. He was buying the evening paper to see what was on. When they get home this evening, they will have forgotten all about what happened today.'

'You are very wise,' said Flop. 'Nothing ever surprises you.'

Bella laughed. 'When you get to my age, you will learn that life is full of surprises.'

'We are learning that already,' said Flip.

'Good,' said Bella. 'Now why don't the two of you have a nice rest?'

'That's a very good idea,' said Flip. He walked over to the dog-door. He pushed it open and stepped inside. He called to Flop, 'Come on, Flop. After all the surprises we had today, you can't be afraid of a dog-door.'

'Of course I'm not afraid of a dog-door,' Flop said. 'And don't you be so bossy. You are getting as bad as Catriona.'

He pushed the dog-door open and jumped into the basket.

Flip said, 'No one could be as bossy as Catriona. And another thing, what she calls surprises and changes we can call adventures!'

'Do you mean that everything that has happened to us today could be called an adventure?'

'Yes,' said Flip.

That made Flop feel much better. He and Flip settled down in their basket and had a lovely sleep.

6
News of Frank

The dogs slept until they heard the sound of two cars coming down the drive. Mr and Mrs Johnson were arriving home at the same time.

Quickly, Flip and Flop went out through the dog-door into the yard. They knew that the Johnsons would be pleased to see them there.

Mr Johnson unlocked the side gate and looked in at them. 'Well, well, well,' he said. 'So you have your dog-door.' He looked at the door.

Mrs Johnson came and joined him. 'What do you think?'

'It looks like a very good job,' he said. 'Let me see the dogs use it. In you go!'

Flip and Flop pushed the door open and went into their room.

'Brilliant!' said Mr Johnson. He locked the side door and opened the front door for himself and Mrs Johnson. 'How did you get on at the golf lesson?'' he asked.

'Not very well, I'm afraid,' she answered.

'Oh well, it's early days yet.' He walked through the house and let Flip and Flop into the kitchen. 'At least you don't have to worry about these two being cooped up while you are out of the house. When is your next lesson?'

'Tomorrow,' said Mrs Johnson.

'Good,' said Mr Johnson. 'The more lessons you have, the sooner you will get the hang of it. I'm hoping to start playing again soon.'

Flip and Flop listened carefully to what was being said.

Then Mr Johnson opened the doors on to the terrace and whistled to the dogs to follow him as he walked around the garden.

'I hope he won't notice where we made the hole bigger,' whispered Flop.

But Mr Johnson didn't seem to notice anything out of place in the garden. When he came back to the terrace, Mrs Johnson said, 'You haven't said a thing about their new look.'

'They look great,' said Mr Johnson. 'Frank won't know them when he sees them! I almost forgot to tell you . . . I had a fax from him at the office. He and Lucy are coming home next Thursday.'

Mrs Johnson wrinkled her brow. 'Next Thursday? That is much sooner than we expected. It can't be half-term already.'

'I think he and Lucy have something important to tell us,' said Mr Johnson.

'It must be very important indeed if they are coming all the way from London.' Mrs Johnson wrinkled her brow again. 'Oh dear, I hope they aren't in any trouble.'

'Somehow I don't think so. I think we might be in for a very pleasant surprise,' said Mr Johnson.

Flip and Flop looked at each other. There was that word again. 'Surprise'!

'Have I time to take the dogs out before supper is ready? It's such a nice evening,' asked Mr Johnson.

'Yes, if they aren't too tired after the excitement of the day,' said Mrs Johnson.

Flip and Flop answered this by rushing to the front door. They sat and wagged their tails and gave little growls and barks.

Mr and Mrs Johnson laughed. Mr Johnson said, 'It is my opinion that those dogs would go for a walk in the middle of the night!'

(And indeed, before very long, that was exactly what Flip and Flop did do.)

But as Mr Johnson put their leads on them,

such an idea was far from the dogs' minds. Instead they were hoping that Bella might be waiting for them at the gate at the top of the drive. They needed to have a long talk with her.

They were not disappointed. Bella was sitting patiently. She ran to meet them. 'Hello, Mr Johnson,' she barked.

'Good dog,' said Mr Johnson.

Then she said to Flip and Flop, 'I wondered if he would take you out. I saw him looking around the garden. Did he notice the hole in the wall?'

'No,' said Flop. 'And neither he nor Mrs Johnson paid any attention to the wire in the yard. We have something more important to tell you. Frank is coming home on Thursday with Lucy. They have something very important to tell Mr and Mrs Johnson.'

'It's a surprise of some kind,' said Flop. 'Mr Johnson said it would be a "pleasant" surprise.'

'That means it will be a nice surprise,' explained Bella.

'Yes, but nice for whom?' asked Flop. He was beginning to feel nervous again. 'I keep remembering what Catriona said this morning about changes happening.'

'Well, there is no good in worrying until you know more,' said Bella. 'Look, there's a rabbit!'

A cheeky-looking rabbit stared at them from a gorse-bush. Then he winked and ran off.

'He knows we are on our leads and can't go after him,' said Flip. 'But, Bella, why don't you chase him?'

'It doesn't seem right to do that while the two of you are so worried,' said Bella.

'We will try not to worry,' promised Flop.

'All right then. I'll go and chase that cheeky rabbit.' Bella went rushing off into the gorse-bushes.

'I suppose you want to go with her,' said Mr Johnson. For the first time ever, he let Flip and Flop off their leads. 'You are to come back when I call.'

This was almost the biggest surprise of the day for Flip and Flop! Mr Johnson letting them off their leads! If Catriona could see what was happening, she would say, 'There you are. I told you there would be changes!'

And that was the last thought that went through the minds of the border terriers before they set off after Bella.

They had no trouble catching up with her.

She took them along dozens of paths used by wild animals. There was no sign of the cheeky rabbit but the dogs snuffled and ran and jumped and barked. They had a wonderful time.

Then Mr Johnson whistled.

'We'd better go back,' said Bella. 'If we don't, he might not let you off the leads again.'

'OK,' said Flip, although he felt that he could go on running for hours and hours.

Mr Johnson put the dogs' leads back on and they all walked very slowly back to the house. At the gate, they met the Rices coming home after the cinema.

Mr Johnson stopped to talk with them. Not a word was said about Flip and Flop being out on the road. Bella said, 'I told you it would be all right. See you in the morning.'

Because the evening was so warm, Mr and Mrs Johnson had their supper on the terrace.

There was a lovely sunset. Flocks of seabirds filled the sky. Neddy neighed in the field next door.

'Oh, the horse is back,' said Mrs Johnson.

Flip and Flop ran down the garden and

called out to him.

Neddy answered them. 'I can't stick my head over the wall now. Mr Johnson gets very cross when I do that. He thinks I am going to eat his roses.'

'And are you going to eat them?' asked Flop.

'No, they are far too prickly,' said Neddy.

'Why were you down in the country all summer?' asked Flop.

'My people take me down there every year,' said Neddy. 'The children take me out riding at their uncle's farm. I have a lovely time. There are other horses for me to talk to and plenty of lovely sweet grass to eat. But now it's late. I'll tell you more tomorrow.'

The dogs ran back to the terrace. Mrs Johnson gave them each a dish of scraps. When they had finished eating, she said, 'Time for bed. We have all had a very busy day!'

As the dogs settled down in their basket, they could hear Mr and Mrs Johnson going around the house locking doors and turning off lights.

'I wonder how many surprises we will have tomorrow,' said Flop as his head began to nod.

'I hope it is twice as many as we had today,' said Flip. His eyes began to close.

Soon the two little dogs were fast asleep but the surprises were far from over. In fact the greatest surprise of all was yet to happen to them.

It began as the moon rose over the hill. It made everything look very strange and lonely. Down at the Quarry Hotel the cats were in the middle of their concert.

'Miaoo,' they sang. 'Miaooo, miaooo . . . Oh how we love to sing to the moon . . .'

Suddenly a bedroom window was opened. A wellington boot was thrown at them. It just missed hitting Catriona. 'Well really,' Catriona said, 'I don't know why I waste my time coming near this place . . .'

'The food was nice,' said one of her friends.

'Yes, it was,' agreed Catriona, jumping down off the bins.

'Where are you going to?' another cat asked.

'I have a little unfinished business to attend to,' said Catriona.

'Who with?' asked the same cat.

'Dogs,' said Catriona.

'Dogs!' cried all the cats together.

A second wellington boot zoomed over their heads. 'Shoo!' an angry voice called. 'Shoo! Shoo! Shoo!'

'Yes,' said Catriona. 'Dogs. But, of course not just any kind of dogs. These are two special dogs that I have decided to help become wise and clever.'

'She must mean Flip and Flop,' said her second friend.

'That's right,' said Catriona. 'They don't always believe what I say to them.'

'Dogs never believe what cats say to them,' said her friend.

'That is why I have decided to show them the world by night,' said Catriona. 'I am going to take them on a journey that they will never forget!'

'Can we come with you?' several cats asked.

'No,' said Catriona. 'You must stay here and keep the humans awake. That will teach them to throw things at us!'

'Very well,' all the cats said together. For some reason that they did not understand, they always did as Catriona told them. It was as though she was their leader. They began to sing again.

More bedroom windows were opened.

More things were thrown at the cats. The hotel manager was awakened by angry guests banging on his bedroom door. 'Do something about those cats!' they called.

Catriona smiled to herself. 'Serves those humans right,' she thought as she slipped across silent gardens and at last reached the yard of the Johnsons' house.

She tapped softly on the dog-door.

She heard Flip and Flop sitting up in their basket.

'Who's there?' Flop asked.

'It's me, Catriona,' said Catriona. 'I've come to show you what happens at night when the humans are all asleep. Just push the door open but don't make too much noise!'

Flip and Flop slipped out through the dog-door as quietly as possible. Catriona looked quite different in the moonlight. Even her smile was different. She said, 'I'll bet you forgot again about using the dog-door to get in and out of the yard. But never mind that for the moment . . . Just follow me.'

'Where are we going?' asked Flop.

'First of all to your back garden. I want to show you that what I said about wild animals being there at night was true.'

Flop was not sure if he felt excited or nervous as he helped Flip to push up the wire at the rockery. He still didn't know as he pushed his way through the scraggly hedge into the field.

'It's an adventure,' he said to himself.

Neddy came sleepily towards them. 'Well I didn't expect to see you so soon again.'

'Lift them into their back garden,' Catriona said.

Silently Flip and Flop followed Neddy to where the garden wall was low. The big horse bent down and gently lifted first Flip and then Flop over the wall into the garden.

Catriona jumped down beside them. They ran quickly to the big bush and lay down in its shadow. 'No animal can see us here,' said Catriona. 'And there's not much wind, so they won't be able to smell us easily.'

A few minutes passed. A cloud drifted across the moon.

When it moved on, the dogs saw a strange creature standing on top of the wall. They knew from what Catriona had told them that morning that it was a fox.

The fox jumped into the garden, paused and listened. It looked up at the moon. Then it stopped and stared at the big bush. Then it dashed across the garden to the gap in the Rices' hedge.

'Foxes are very clever,' Catriona said. 'That one saw us at once. But look at the badger!'

A beautiful black and white animal was nosing its way through the hole by the rose-bush.

'It's never come in that way before,' said Catriona.

'I made the hole bigger today,' said Flip. He was trembling all over. So was Flop. Neither of them knew why they hadn't gone running after the fox. They had wanted to, just as now they wanted to run at the badger.

'It's all very strange,' thought Flip.

'Maybe it is because it is night-time,' thought Flop.

Then they both thought, 'Maybe it has something to do with Catriona! Maybe she is the Queen of the Night!'

The badger moved slowly around the garden, digging little holes here and there.

Flip forgot about being quiet and said, 'I hope we won't get blamed for that.'

The badger tensed and disappeared.

After that nothing happened.

Then Catriona said, 'This is boring!' Why don't we go up to the park on the top of the hill?'

'In the middle of the night?' Flop managed to say.

'Yes,' said Catriona. She ran and called to Neddy. 'Lift the dogs back over, please.'

Neddy did as he was asked. 'Now I suppose you'll go back to bed.'

'No,' said Flip. 'Catriona is going to take us to the park on the hill.'

'I don't think that is such a good idea,' said Neddy.

But Flip and Flop were not listening to him. They were running after Catriona.

She was already half way through the scraggly hedge. Then she ran up the drive towards the gate.

7

After Dark on the Hill

Catriona jumped up on to the wall that surrounded the first of the small houses on the road down to the village. She found it easier to run along the tops of the walls than to stay on the road.

She looked behind to make sure that Flip and Flop were following her.

She felt quite proud when she saw how quietly and quickly they were running along the road. They moved like shadows in and out of the parked cars and reached the end of the narrow road at almost the same time as she did.

Here the three animals paused and looked to the left, then to the right, then to the left again. It was too late for there to be much traffic on the road. All the same, they knew it was stupid to take chances crossing the main road. No matter what time it was, a car or a motor-cycle could come speeding around the corner.

No car or motor-bike did come around the corner but the pause gave Flip and Flop the chance to think how strange everything looked by moonlight.

They knew the road very well. They also knew the steps into the park very well too. They had often been there with the Johnsons during the day. Now it was all changed.

The steps looked white and cold. The trees that grew on the hill looked like big leafy monsters.

'All right, it is safe to cross,' Catriona said.

Once more, Flip and Flop followed her. They ran up the steps. From there they followed the path to the top of the hill. Here there were no trees, just a strange stone shape that humans called 'a monument'. In fine weather humans often sat here and looked at the sea and the mountains.

But there were no humans around now. Instead the grass that surrounded the monument was covered by dozens of rabbits.

They hopped here. They hopped there. They seemed to hop everywhere. They only stopped hopping to sniff noses or to nibble at the grass.

Catriona nodded to the dogs to hide behind a bush.

'They come out at night when the moon is this bright,' she whispered.

'Do you never chase them?' Flip whispered back.

'Sometimes,' Catriona replied.

'Will we chase them now?' asked Flip.

'I don't think we have to,' said Catriona. 'Look over there.'

A thin shape was moving through a tangle of long grass close to where the rabbits were.

Suddenly the rabbits saw it. They dashed off in all directions as the shape rushed out into the moonlight. It was long and thin with sharp white teeth.

It moved faster even than Catriona but it was not fast enough to catch any of the rabbits. They all ran down into the rabbit warrens on the other side of some rocks.

The wicked-looking little animal turned around and glared at the cat and the two dogs. Then, without making a sound, it vanished back into the long grass.

'What was that?' asked Flop.

'That was a stoat,' said Catriona. 'Never go near one if you can help it. A stoat can give you a terrible bite.'

'Maybe we should go on home now,' said Flop. He was feeling nervous again.

'Of course not,' said Catriona. 'No one will come near us, not while there are three of us.'

She moved on down the other side of the
hill. Flip went after her. Flop had a quick
look around to make sure that nothing was
following him. Then he caught up with Flip.
Anything was better than being left alone by
the monument.

Catriona led them away from the main
paths. She followed tracks that took them
through bushes and pools of water and old
ruined buildings. Flip thought that he and
Flop had seen some of these before on their
walks with Frank but he could not be sure.

Flop was almost too afraid to look around
him. The whole hill was alive with the sound

of animals moving in the shadows.

Catriona would sometimes stop and say, 'That was a fox . . .' or 'That was a rat . . .' or 'That was a mouse . . .'

But the dogs just were not fast enough to see anything, except a sudden tremble in the gorse or the long grass. Once or twice they got a very strong smell that they knew must be an animal whose name even Catriona did not know.

Then suddenly they came out from under the trees. In front of them was another ruin. The dogs knew at once what it was. It was the old castle on the other side of the hill. Frank had sheltered here one day when it had rained.

'So you know where you are now, do you?' asked Catriona. She could see that Flop was not so nervous now.

'Yes,' said Flop. He sighed a big sigh of relief. 'We can go home if we go down this path.'

'First we have to visit the quarry,' Catriona said. 'Have you ever been there?'

'I don't think so,' said Flip.

'Could we not leave it for another night?' asked Flop. He felt that they had done enough exploring for the time being.

'It won't take very long,' Catriona promised. 'And it is kind of on the way back to your house.'

The path down to the quarry was one of the narrowest that the dogs had ever walked along. 'I don't think we have ever been here before,' said Flip. 'I don't think that even Frank could walk on this path.'

'Humans usually come a different way. They take the road to the hotel,' said Catriona. 'Except of course those that come out here to climb the quarry.'

Climb the quarry? The dogs were amazed! Why would anyone want to climb the quarry?

'Humans do it so that later on they can climb mountains,' explained Catriona. 'They use ropes and special shoes and climb up and down the sides of the quarry.'

The sides of the quarry looked very high and hard. They were made of solid rock with just a few clumps of grass and wild flowers growing on them.

'It must be very dangerous,' said Flop.

'Not if you know what you are doing,' said Catriona.

'Have you ever climbed the quarry?' asked Flip.

'Of course not,' said Catriona. 'I only climb things when I have to. Cats can get stuck as well. I know one cat who got stuck up a tree. The fire-brigade had to be sent for to get her back down.'

'We certainly are learning a lot of things tonight,' Flip thought as they reached the end of the narrow path and stepped out on nice flat ground.

'Now listen,' said Catriona.

Flip and Flop listened.

At first, they could hear nothing. Then they heard dozens of sounds like the ones they had heard on the hill.

'More wild animals,' Catriona said. 'They come to drink from the pool of water at the edge of the quarry.'

A different sound made the cat and the dogs look up.

A great wide-winged bird flew over their heads.

'That's an owl out hunting,' said Catriona.

The owl swooped down. There was a squeak. Then the owl flew back into the sky. There was something in its claws.

'I think it's caught a mouse,' said Catriona.

Flip and Flop shivered. The thought of hunting for things to eat filled them with excitement. Then that feeling vanished as something came crashing out of the bushes at the foot of the quarry.

There was a great scampering to be heard as all the wild animals raced away to safety.

'Now where did that dog come from?' Catriona demanded angrily.

Flip and Flop looked more carefully at the black and white shape rushing around the edge of the pool. Not only was it a dog but it was a dog that they knew. It was Sam-Boy!

'Sam-Boy!' Flip called.

Sam-Boy skidded to a halt. 'So we meet again,' he said. 'Is that a cat you have with you?'

'Yes, it's Catriona,' said Flop. 'But what are you doing here all by yourself in the middle of the night?'

Sam-Boy said, 'To tell you the truth, I'm lost.'

'That means that he can't find his way

home,' said Catriona. 'But it does not give him the right to frighten all the wild animals.'

'I was hungry,' said Sam-Boy.

'You should have gone to the Quarry Hotel if you want something to eat,' said Catriona.

'Is she joking?' Sam-Boy asked the border terriers.

'No,' said Flop 'There was a wedding there today and . . .'

'Don't waste time talking,' said Catriona. 'Let's just show him.' She didn't really like talking to Sam-Boy. The only dog, apart from Flip and Flop, that she had ever spoken to was Bella. If she wasn't careful, she would end up talking to every dog that came along. With swish of her tail, she walked away from the quarry. This time she did not look back to see if the dogs were following her. But she knew that they would not stay at the quarry by themselves.

The dogs talked as they followed Catriona.

'How did you get lost?' Flip asked.

Sam-Boy said, 'After I left you, I just kept on walking and walking. I met dozens of other dogs and talked to them. I just wasn't thinking of where I was going. Then it started to get dark. I didn't know where I was.'

'Maybe you'll remember how to get home when you've had something to eat,' said Flop.

The Quarry Hotel was all in darkness. The cats had finished their concert hours ago. The guests and the manager were sound asleep. Catriona took the dogs to where the bins were. 'No noise, please,' she said. 'Just take whatever you want to eat.'

'And how can I manage that?' asked Sam-Boy.

'Just by looking inside the bins,' said Catriona. Then she sighed deeply as she realised that Sam-Boy could not do this. The hotel bins were not like the ones that humans have in their houses.

The hotel bins were big metal bins, as tall as a human. A cat could manage to jump into them. A dog had no chance of doing this. To make matters worse, the hotel manager had put heavy lids on top of the bins to stop the cats from getting at the scraps. He hoped this would keep them away.

'It looks as though I am going to have to stay hungry,' said Sam-Boy, 'unless I try and eat those wellington boots. I wonder who threw those away. The one over there looks brand-new.'

'So does this one here,' said Flip, sniffing the boot next to him.

'Never mind the boots,' Catriona said quickly. 'We will have to think of something else.'

Before that could happen, there was a swishing noise from the darkness of the hotels grounds. First one cat. Then another. Then another. Then another. They all came forward to where Catriona and the dogs stood.

'We are amazed at you, Catriona,' they said. 'We are surprised and amazed. We heard you were up on the hill. We were going to look for you. We did not know that you were with three dogs!'

'I started out with these two called Flip and Flop. I was proving to them that what I said about the wild animals being out at night was true,' Catriona replied. 'This third dog is a friend of theirs. He is lost.'

'Dogs are always getting lost,' said a black cat. 'They are stupid.'

'You watch what you are saying,' snarled Sam-Boy.

Flip and Flop began to growl angrily.

Catriona said in a voice that made all the animals quiet. 'Let's prove that cats are more clever than dogs. Let us find out where Sam-Boy lives!'

'He came out along the road by the river,' said a yellow cat. 'I saw him as I was coming here for the concert.'

'I saw him before that,' said a grey cat. 'He was coming along the road from the shopping centre.'

'I know how to get to my home from the shopping centre,' said Sam-Boy. 'That is if it's the shopping centre with the swings for children around the back.'

'That is exactly the shopping centre that I mean,' said the grey cat.

'Then take him there,' said Catriona.

The grey cat did not look very pleased but Catriona looked so determined that the grey cat said, 'Oh all right. Come on, dog!'

'Thanks very much,' Sam-Boy said to Catriona. 'Sorry to be a trouble.' To Flip and Flop he said, 'See you soon.'

Then he had to run after the grey cat who was already gone from the bins.

'I'd better take Flip and Flop home,' said Catriona.

By now, even Flip had had enough surprises for one night. He was glad to go off with Flop and Catriona.

He was even more glad when he and Flop slipped under the wire, through the dog-door and into their basket. 'Won't Bella be amazed?' he said as he settled down to sleep.

Back at the hotel, the rest of the cats were having a terrible quarrel over Catriona bringing the dogs to the bins.

Some of the cats said she had no right to do such a thing.

Others said she was right to show the dogs how clever cats were.

Then the guests woke up again. And so did the manager. This time they did not just throw boots at the cats. They all rushed downstairs in their nightclothes and chased the cats away.

The cats never went back to the hotel again.

8

The Storm

Next morning, as soon as they were let out into the garden, Flip and Flop rushed off to talk to Bella.

They met her getting through the gap in the hedge.

'Hello,' she said. 'Do you know that I had the strangest dream last night? I dreamt that I heard the two of you running up the drive after Mr and Mrs Johnson went to bed.'

Flip and Flop gave little barks of delight and rushed around the big bush for several minutes before they told Bella what had happened to them.

Bella listened in amazement. 'So it wasn't a dream at all,' she said. 'You really did go up the hill in the middle of the night!'

Neddy said from the other side of the wall, 'I told them not to, but they wouldn't listen.'

'And are they not right not to listen to you?' Catriona was back in her usual place on the wall. 'They would have missed the biggest adventure of their lives.'

'They could also have got into trouble,'

said Bella. 'I hope you will not do anything as silly as that again.'

'Oh don't worry,' said Catriona. 'I won't go walking on the hill at night for a long time. The Indian summer is over.'

'What do you mean by the "Indian" summer?' asked Flip.

'Before I answer that question, I would just like to say that I think it is very sensible of you to talk to me without getting all uptight,' said Catriona.

'What does "uptight" mean?' asked Flop.

'It means getting cross when there is no need to,' said Catriona. 'I know it is unusual for cats and dogs to be best friends. But I think that, in our case, we should be able to say that we are best friends. I have, after all, known you almost since the first day you arrived in Ireland.'

'You've known Bella even longer than that!' said Flip. 'Why aren't you and she best friends?'

'Perhaps we are but Bella doesn't like to say it,' said Catriona.

Bella made a sound that was half a bark and half a growl.

'None of us knows what that sound means,' said Catriona.

'It means that I would not mind being your friend if you would just not be so annoying,' said Bella.

'I'll do my best not to annoy you in future,' said Catriona. 'And you must remember that I am a cat. Cats have their own ways of saying and doing things.'

'So do horses,' said Neddy, sticking his head over the wall.

'What if Mr Johnson sees you?' asked Flop, remembering about the rose-bushes.

'He's just driven off to the office,' said Neddy.

'He's late,' said Catriona. 'That's what I meant about the end of the Indian summer.'

'Please, Catriona,' said Bella. 'You said you would not try to annoy us. Yet that is what you are doing. You are talking in riddles.'

'Then, let me explain as best as I can what I mean by the end of the Indian summer,' said Catriona. 'Flip and Flop had to leave the mountains because of the flood caused by the rain. Is that not true?'

'Yes, it is,' said Flip and Flop.

'But since you came down here, the weather has been very good, has it not?' continued Catriona.

Flip and Flop nodded.

'Yet the summer should have finished weeks ago. Instead we have had what humans call an "Indian" summer. This means that the summer didn't finish after the big rain storm. It just went on and on and on. The sunshine woke Mr and Mrs Johnson every morning. They got so used to it that they didn't even set their alarm-clock.'

'How could you possibly know that?' asked Bella.

'I often lie on the ledge of their bedroom window first thing in the morning,' said Catriona. 'It's a perfect way to begin the day. I'd have heard the alarm go off while I was there. Instead what I hear is Mrs Johnson saying. "Time for us to rise and shine like the sun coming in through the windows" '.

The other animals looked at each other. They were all wondering if Catriona was making all this up. But before they could decide, Catriona said, 'This morning things are different. There is no sun.'

The other animals looked up in the sky. It was filled with grey clouds.

'So Mr and Mrs Johnson slept longer than usual. That is why Mr Johnson was late.'

Neddy said, 'I've never heard of humans who didn't use an alarm-clock or a radio or something to wake them up.'

'Well, that just goes to show that not all humans are the same' said Catriona. 'Flip and Flop would do well to remember that. They would also do well to remember what I said to them only yesterday about changes happening. A very big change might be about to happen now.'

'And what's that?' asked Bella, cross with Catriona, whose words were making Flip and Flop feel very nervous.

'The beginning of autumn,' said Catriona.

'Autumn begins every year,' said Neddy. 'First we have spring when things begin to grow. Then we have summer, when things begin to ripen and I go down the country. Then we have the autumn, when things are ready to eat. Then we have the winter, when things get very cold.'

'That's right,' said Bella. 'Autumn comes every year.'

'Ah but this year it will be different because the fine summer weather has gone on for so long,' said Catriona. 'Autumn will come suddenly.'

'Suddenly? Do you mean today?' Flip asked. His voice sounded shivery.

'Yes, it could happen today,' said Catriona.

'I hope you and Flop won't catch cold. I am amazed that Mr and Mrs Johnson should have left it so late before they had your coats cut.'

'You didn't say that yesterday,' said Bella. 'You told them that they looked nice.'

'Yes, I know that I did. But I had forgotten all about autumn. Maybe Mr and Mrs Johnson forgot about it too. Maybe they thought that the fine weather would go on for ever and ever,' said Catriona. 'But it was a good thing that I took Flip and Flop up on the hill last night. It will be the last chance to go there for ages and ages. Now, if you will excuse me, I have to go and meet the cats who were at the concert at the Quarry Hotel. It seems that some of them are still quite cross because I brought dogs there.'

She got ready to jump down off the wall into the next garden. Then she remembered something. 'Oh by the way, I heard from the grey cat that Sam-Boy got home safely.'

With that she vanished from sight.

Neddy said, 'I don't know what to make of all that.'

'Neither do I,' said Bella.

Suddenly a gust of wind blew in off the sea. It shook the branches of all the trees.

Leaves fell off and landed on top of the dogs.

'Is this how autumn begins?' Flop was trembling all over now.

Before Bella could answer, there was another gust of wind that lasted for several minutes. This gust made the trees and the rose-bushes bend. It sent even more leaves blowing like pieces of paper across the grass.

Then the rain began. It came down in huge drops. Within seconds, the whole garden was soaking wet. So too were the dogs as the rain slid off the big bush and on top of them.

'This is the way the storm began in the mountains,' said Flip.

'You don't think it will break the house like it broke the cottage, do you?' Flop asked.

'It was the shed falling on it that broke the cottage,' said Flip.

'The garden shed here is very close to this house,' said Flop.

'Now, now,' said Bella. 'You are getting upset over nothing at all. I am sure that my house and your house are much better built than the cottage in the mountains. And if the garden shed did blow down, it would fall into the yard. It wouldn't even touch the house.'

'Bella is right,' said Neddy. 'You have no

need to worry.'

Just then Mrs Johnson came out on to the terrace and called Flip and Flop. Bella came with them to see what she wanted.

'I think you should come in out of that rain,' she said. 'We are in for a terrible storm. Bella, you can come in as well for a while. I'll just telephone Mr and Mrs Rice and tell them where you are.'

The dogs settled down on the rug in front of the fire.

It was only the second time that Mrs Johnson had lit a fire since Flip and Flop had come to live in the house.

She had also switched on several lights in the living-room.

'You would think it was the end of the day instead of the beginning,' said Flip.

From where they sat, they could see out into the garden. The wind blew across it now without stopping. As well as leaves from the trees, flowers from the rose-bushes were being scattered all over the place.

The sea, far down below, was as grey as the sky. Big white waves crashed on to the beach.

It was hard to imagine how quiet and hot the beach had been the last time they had been there with Frank.

'The bay will be full of seaweed in the morning,' said Flip. 'Not that we will get to see it!'

'There might be another dead seabird on the rocks,' said Flop. 'I hope Catriona is all right.'

'She will know plenty of places to shelter,' said Bella.

'Where exactly does she live?' asked Flip.

'In a big dark house,' said Bella.

'What are her humans like?' asked Flop.

'Old,' said Bella. 'My humans go and see them sometimes. They took me with them once.'

'I wonder if that is why Catriona is always wandering around,' said Flop. 'Maybe she doesn't like living in a dark old house.'

'Cats can be very strange,' said Bella. 'But I think Catriona is the strangest one that I have ever met.'

9

A Terrible Accident

'Dear, oh dear, what a terrible storm!' said Mrs Johnson. 'And for it to happen so quickly! And, of course, the weather would change just as I started my golf lessons! Well, they will have to wait now!'

Flip and Flop felt much better when they heard this. It meant that they wouldn't have to spend hours and hours in the yard.

Of course if they got bored, they could always lift the wire and get out into the rockery . . .

But, no, they both told themselves, they mustn't even think about more adventures, especially while the weather was so bad.

And really they were very happy as they were, in front of the fire with Bella. They could have a nice long talk about all that had happened to them since they had left Scotland. But, before they could even start, Mrs Johnson got out the vacuum cleaner.

Bella said, 'I think maybe I'll go home . . .'

She went to the door and barked.

Mrs Johnson laughed, 'Now don't tell me

you hate the vacuum cleaner as much as Flip and Flop! All right so! Out you go!'

She opened the door just wide enough for Bella to slip out. Flip and Flop watched as she ran to the gap in the hedge. The wind was so strong that it almost blew her over. But she made it safely to the hedge and home.

Mrs Johnson switched on the vacuum cleaner. Every time it came near them, Flip and Flop barked at it.

When she had finished the living-room, Mrs Johnson said, 'I may as well get Frank's room ready and the guest-room for Lucy. They will be here the day after tomorrow.'

The day after tomorrow! The dogs hadn't realised that it would be as soon as that.

In spite of not liking the vacuum cleaner, they followed Mrs Johnson when she went upstairs. She might say something else about Frank. Also they had never, never been allowed upstairs before. But they thought that Mrs Johnson might allow them up this morning. She was in a very friendly mood.

'He'll be delighted to see the two of you. He asks for you every time he writes. Did I tell you that before?' Then she smiled at Flip and Flop. 'Will you just listen to me talking to two dogs as though they were humans!'

Flip and Flop wagged their tails.

Then they went ahead of Mrs Johnson on to the landing. A corridor, leading to the bedrooms, stretched before them.

The doors to all the bedrooms were open. They saw Harry's trainers under a chair so they knew that that was his room. Then they saw Joan's tennis-racquet against the wall in another room so they knew that that was Joan's room.

Mr and Mrs Johnson's room they knew because the bed had not yet been made.

In Frank's room there were neat piles of typed sheets of paper on a table in front of the window. Several pairs of shoes were lined up under the dressing-table. Flip and Flop hurried over to sniff them.

They still smelled of the hill and the beach and all the other places that they had been to with Frank.

Mrs Johnson said, 'You are going to have to put up with the vacuum-cleaner again.' She plugged in the machine.

There was an extra strong gust of wind off the sea. Then there was a loud crash from the back yard. Flip and Flop scuttled into a corner of the room. Mrs Johnson said, 'What on earth was that?'

She hurried towards the window. As she did so, her feet got tangled in the flex of the vacuum-cleaner. To the dogs' horror, she fell forward and banged her head off the side of the table.

For a moment it was as if the whole world stood still. Then Flip and Flop rushed forward. They each licked Mrs Johnson's hand. She didn't move. She just lay there. Her face was very white.

'What are we going to do?' asked Flip.

'We will have to get help like you did when I got caught on that branch. Do you remember how I nearly choked?' said Flop.

'Of course I do,' said Flip. 'Bella made Mr and Mrs Rice come and rescue you. We have to make them come in to help Mrs Johnson!'

The dogs rushed downstairs, into the kitchen and out through the dog-door. The crash they had heard had been the sound of the wire fence being blown down.

The wire and the strong wooden poles now lay on top of the rockery. Carefully the dogs walked over it and went through the scraggly hedge into the field.

'We'll need Neddy to lift us into the garden,' said Flop.

But there was no sign of the horse. 'His

humans must have taken him in out of the storm,' said Flip. 'We will just have to go to the front door of the Rices' house and hope that Bella will hear us.'

'No, we won't,' said Flop. 'Look what's happened to the garden wall.'

The part of the garden wall where the hole was had fallen into the field.

'The rain did that,' said Flip. 'The hole must have helped to loosen the stones.'

The dogs scrambled over the pile of stones and clay. The rain poured down on them, making it very hard not to slip back down into the field. Or, worse, bring more of the wall down on top of them!

But, somehow, they managed it and ran across the garden to the gap in the hedge.

The grass was so wet that crossing it was like paddling in a stream.

They reached the back door of the house and began to bark as loudly as they could.

The wind whistled around them. The rain pattered down.

'They will never hear us with all this noise,' said Flip.

'Maybe if they could *see* us,' said Flop. 'I'm going to try and jump the way that Sam-Boy showed us.' He ran a few metres away from

the kitchen window. Then he stood quite still. Then he flung himself forward and forced his feet to leave the ground. To his delight and Flip's amazement, he actually rose high enough in the air to bang against the window.

Mrs Rice was in the kitchen, drinking tea. She gave a loud scream when she saw Flop appear as if out of nowhere.

Mr Rice stopped what he was doing and ran into the kitchen with Bella at his heels. 'What's wrong?' he asked.

'Flop is outside. I think the wind blew him against the window!'

'Then we had better let him in!'

Mr and Mrs Rice opened the back door.

Bella said, 'Oh, so you are both here!'

'Mrs Johnson needs help,' said Flip.

'Come on in, little dogs,' Mrs Rice said.

'Tell her we can't,' said Flip.

'I would if I thought they would understand,' said Bella.

'They have to follow us,' said Flop.

'I don't think they will go in all this wind and rain,' said Bella. 'Anyway they would never fit through the gap in the hedge!'

'Then they will have to come out through the front door,' said Flop. He ran past Bella and the Rices and into the hall.

Flip followed. Then Bella joined them. They all barked as loudly as they could.

'They've gone mad!' said Mr Rice. 'The storm has driven them mad!'

'I don't think so,' said Mrs Rice, reaching for the telephone. 'Bella has never carried on like this before because of a storm.' She dialled the Johnsons' number and listened to the ringing sound. 'No one is answering. Yet I know that Mrs Johnson is there. Frank's car is parked outside. She would never go out in this weather without taking the car.'

'You are right,' said Mr Rice.

Quickly he and Mrs Rice put on their raincoats and hats and hurried to the Johnsons' house. They rang the doorbell and banged with the knocker. There was no reply.

Flip and Flop tugged at Mr Rice's coat. 'They want me to follow them,' he said.

The border terriers led him across the rockery and through the scraggly hedge into the field.

From there they brought him to where the wall had collapsed.

'I just hope this turns out to be something important,' he said as he slipped and slid over the stones and the clay that the rain had turned into mud. His coat and shoes and trousers were covered in dark wet stains.

When he was safely in the garden, he understood what Flip and Flop were doing. 'Of course! The doors on to the terrace aren't locked! I can get into the house that way!'

He quickly slid the glass doors back, stepped into the living-room and called out, 'Mrs Johnson? Are you here, Mrs Johnson?'

Flip and Flop barked again. Mr Rice followed them out into the hall. He opened the front door and let Mrs Rice and Bella in.

'She's upstairs,' Flip said to Bella.

'Lead the way,' said Bella.

The humans and Bella followed Flip and Flop up to Frank's room. Mrs Johnson was still lying on the floor.

'What on earth could have happened?' Mrs Rice asked.

Mrs Johnson gave a little groan and opened her eyes.

'Don't move,' said Mrs Rice.

'I'm all right really.' Mrs Johnson sat up.

'You have a terrible bruise,' said Mrs Rice.

'How did you know that I fell?'

'Flip and Flop came and told us,' said Mr Rice. 'Now I'll go and telephone the doctor.'

10
Frank and Lucy Come Home

By the time the doctor arrived, Mrs Johnson was sitting in the chair at Frank's table. She still looked very white. The bruise on her forehead was getting blacker and blacker. She also had a lump over one eye.

'You were very lucky that you didn't hit yourself off the sharp edge of the table,' the doctor said.

'I was also very lucky to have two very clever little dogs in the house,' said Mrs Johnson. 'They saved Frank when they were living in the mountains. Now they helped to save me.'

The doctor smiled. 'What kind of dogs are they?'

'Border terriers,' said Mrs Johnson.

'I might think of getting one for my family,' he said. 'Now I want you to do absolutely nothing for the rest of the day. I am leaving you some tablets. You are bound to have a headache later on.'

'I am also going to look as though I was in a fight,' said Mrs Johnson. 'I don't know what my husband is going to say.'

'I will telephone Mr Johnson and explain what happened,' said the Doctor.

'And I'm going to put away this vacuum cleaner and make us all a nice cup of tea,' said Mrs Rice. 'I spilled the last one I was drinking when Flop appeared at the window. Do you know that, for a second I thought the wind was blowing him away!'

'Talking of things being blown away,' said Mrs Johnson as she went to lie down in her own room. 'What was that terrible crash that I heard just before I fell?'

'It was the wire fencing in the yard coming down,' said Mr Rice. 'Part of the wall into the field collapsed as well. But these things are easily fixed. I'll be happy to give your husband a hand.'

Mr Johnson came home from the office as soon as he heard about his wife's accident. He was delighted that she had not hurt herself too badly. All the same, he insisted that she stay in bed. He said, 'I will heat some soup for our lunch.'

'Thank you,' said Mrs Johnson. 'Oh and don't forget to thank Flip and Flop too.'

'They deserve two dog-biscuits each,' said Mr Johnson.

'And so does Bella,' said Mrs Johnson.

In all the excitement, the Rices had forgotten to take Bella back with them. She had stayed out on the landing while the doctor had examined Mrs Johnson. Now she was sitting at the door of the bedroom with Flip and Flop.

'Yes, I'll give Bella some biscuits as well. But first of all, all dogs must go downstairs. The place is covered with mud,' said Mr Johnson.

'Mr Rice brought most of that in on his shoes,' said Mrs Johnson. 'Such a pity! I was just getting Frank's room ready.'

'Frank's room is fine,' said Mr Johnson. 'And the storm seems to have stopped. I think the sun is trying to shine through.'

And so it was, in a very weak sort of way.

The dogs ate their biscuits in the kitchen. Then they went out into the garden through the terrace doors that Mr Rice hadn't bothered to close.

'We could go anywhere we want to now,' said Flip. 'The wall into the field won't be mended until tomorrow at the earliest.'

'I'm going to stay close to home,' said Bella. 'I've had enough excitement for one day. You should do the same thing. You don't want to get into trouble just as the Johnsons think you are the best dogs in the world.'

'That's true,' said Flip.

So he and Flop sat and watched the garden drying. By afternoon the raindrops had stopped falling off the trees. Neddy came galloping up the field. 'I hear that I missed all the excitement,' he said. 'My humans took me in out of the storm. Did you really save Mrs Johnson's life?'

'Now who told you that?' asked Flip.

Bella said, 'I'll bet it was Catriona.'

'Yes,' said Neddy.

'And we never saw her at all while it was all happening,' said Flop.

'Would you like to come for a ride?' asked Neddy.

'Do you mean on your back?' asked Bella.

'Yes,' said Neddy. 'There is a dog called Mac on the farm who often goes for a gallop with the humans.'

'But not by himself,' said Bella. 'He has a human to help him stay on.'

'You are right, of course,' said Neddy. 'Maybe when Frank comes back he will get a horse.'

'We could play racing,' said Bella.

'Of course we could,' said Neddy. 'Around and around the field would be great!'

So the three dogs scrambled into the field and began to race and race around the field after Neddy. Running through the wet grass wiped all the mud off them.

Then Bella said, 'I'm out of breath.'

And Flop said, 'Maybe Flip and I should go back into the house while we are nice and clean.'

They went through the scraggly hedge, across the rockery and in through the dog-door. They settled down and had a nice sleep. When they woke up, they were as clean as when they had left Mrs Joyce's house.

They managed to stay clean all that day and all the next day too. Mrs Johnson was well enough to get out of bed but not to take the dogs for a walk. Mr Johnson didn't have time. He and Mr Rice were too busy mending the wire fence and the wall.

They finished the work just a few hours before it was time to go and meet Frank and Lucy at the airport.

Flip and Flop sat and waited in the yard for the sound of the car coming down the drive.

When at last they heard it, they just couldn't stop barking. Then they rushed into their room and waited for the door to open. They heard Frank's voice in the kitchen. The key turned in the lock. The door opened. There was Frank exactly as they remembered him.

'Hello, hello,' he said. 'I've been hearing all about you on the way home from the airport.'

A very pretty woman with long hair came and looked at Flip and Flop. 'I'm Lucy,' she said. 'It was I who had you sent to Frank from Scotland.'

Lucy and Frank gave the dogs such a petting that they thought they would die from happiness.

Then Mrs Johnson said, 'Now before you do anything else, I want the two of you to come and sit down in the living room and tell us what your surprise is.'

Flip and Flop followed the humans into the living-room and settled down at Frank's feet.

'Well,' said Frank, 'the surprise is first of all that my book is going to be published.'

'That's great,' said Mr Johnson.

'And the second part of the surprise is that

they want me to write a second book,' said Frank.

'Better and better,' said Mr Johnson.

'And the third part of the surprise is that we have been given a cottage down in County Kerry,' said Lucy. 'An aunt of mine bought it years ago and now she doesn't want it any more. She is giving it to us as a wedding present.'

'Does that mean you are coming back to live in Ireland?' asked Mrs Johnson.

'Yes, it does,' said Lucy. 'Of course I might have to go away now and again if I get parts in films or TV series, but Frank and I want to go and live in Kerry. He can write his second book there.'

'And maybe get work making furniture,' said Frank. 'We are planning to get married next month in Dublin.'

'I only hope my bruise will have gone by then,' said Mrs Johnson.

That made everyone laugh. Then the humans all hugged each other and began to talk about letting Lucy's parents, who lived in America, know what was going to happen.

'And Joan and Harry have to be told as well,' said Mrs Johnson. Then she looked at

Flip and Flop. 'What about the dogs?'

'They will come with us to Kerry,' Frank said.

'We will miss them,' said his father.

'That's a change!' said Frank. 'You didn't even like them at first!'

'I know,' said Mr Johnson. 'But I like them now!'

'Well then, why don't we get two border terriers for ourselves?' asked Mrs Johnson. 'The doctor said he might get one too.'

So it looked as though there would always be border terriers in the house on the hill by the sea.

'Wait till we tell Bella all this news,' said Flip.

'I'll bet that Catriona is already doing that,' said Flop.

This is the third Flip 'n' Flop book. The others are:

Flip 'n' Flop
In which the two little border terriers – Flip who is 'for ever flipping around the place, trying to find out what things are about' and Flop who is 'for ever flopping over and wanting to sleep' – come all the way from Scotland to start a new life with Frank in the Wicklow hills.

About their friends and enemies, and their moment of high drama when the floods come . . .

More about Flip 'n' Flop
In which the two terriers come to live above Killiney Bay, sample the delights of swimming and fishing, take exciting walks through new unexplored territory, learn about old hunting techniques and exchange experiences at that best of all animal clubs – the vet's.

But can they come to terms with the cat next door (Catriona) and Frank's father who just doesn't seem to like them . . .?